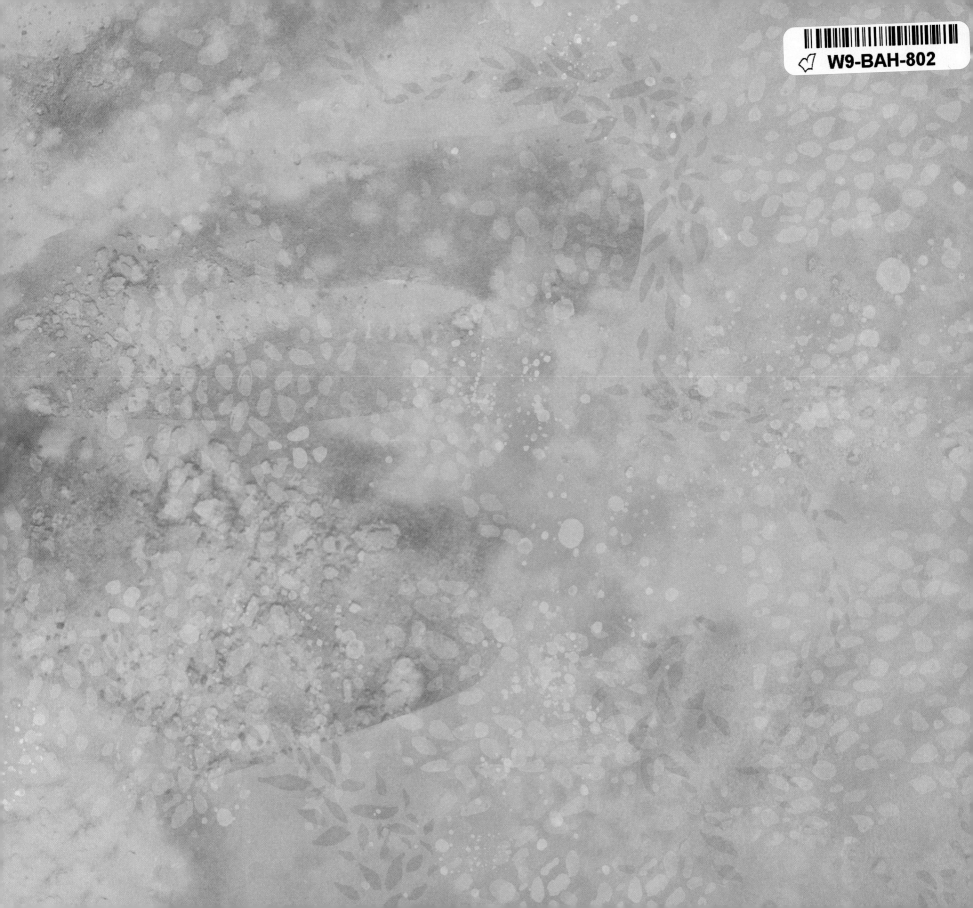

The Best Bed for Me

GAIA CORNWALL

CANDLEWICK PRESS

"Time for bed, Sweet Pea," my mama says.
"Where's my tree?"
"Tree?"

"I want to sleep high up in a tree like the koalas!"

"OK, good night, little koala," my mama says.

"Or maybe I'll sleep like . . .

"a sea otter! We could hold hands all night long."

"You do love to snuggle, little otter. Now time for—"

"You know who else loves to snuggle, Mama?

"Piglets! They curl up in the mud."

"Piglet," my mama says,
"you must be tired. Let's—"
"It might be too muddy. Maybe I'll sleep cuddled down like . . .

"a puffin! A burrow will be nice and dry."

"Thank goodness I have a burrow right here for you!"

"But I think it's too small. I need to stretch out . . .

"like a whale in the ocean!
They keep swimming even when they sleep!"

"Well, you are a good swimmer.

How 'bout you float right under these blankets,
my whale," says my mama.

"But I don't know if I can swim all night long.

Maybe I could sleep upside down like . . .

"a bat! They hold on with their feet
and hang down from branches."

"My little bat, it's time to calm our bodies down."

"Maybe it would be relaxing to sleep standing up!
Like an . . .

"emperor penguin! Oh, they're my favorite! They don't even let their toes touch the ground."

"Little penguin, do you know how my favorite sleeps?"
"What is your favorite, Mama?"

"You. You're my favorite."

"Well, I sleep in this big-kid bed, with a soft pillow and a fluffy blanket. It's the best bed for me."

"Good night, Sweet Pea."
"Good night, Mama."
"Sweet dreams."

I created the bulk of this book during a year of COVID upheaval. And so it seems especially fitting that I dedicate it, with my whole heart, to parents and caregivers everywhere, especially at bedtime when **everyone** *is exhausted. May we channel Mama's patience and all have meltdown-free nights forevermore. We certainly deserve them.*

This book was typeset in Mrs. Eaves. The illustrations were done in pencil and watercolor, then colored digitally.
Candlewick Press, 99 Dover Street, Somerville, Massachusetts 02144. www.candlewick.com.
Printed in Vicenza, Italy. 22 23 24 25 26 27 LGO 10 9 8 7 6 5 4 3 2 1